Kamikaze of Songs
By Mianne Adufutse

Kamikaze of Songs

Mianne Adufutse

Mi Books
©2009

Kamikaze of Songs

Mianne Adufutse

because beautiful things do not always rhyme

Kamikaze of Songs

Mianne Adufutse

Pretty Talker

Your lips are dripping in their kool-aid lies,
Your lips are drowning in their new age guise

Kamikaze of Songs

Last Year's Anthem (Lyrics)

Don't ask me to
I ain't doing nothing with you
so don't you keep asking me to
--said I ain't doing nothing with you

See,
you be the type of guy
--you know the one the ones that be acting all fly,
minute I give you a go
you start hanging in the streets like a hoe

Your loves the kind of cruel,
turn a good girl to a real big fool
so, no, no
I ain't doing nothing with you
waste your time keep asking me to

Mianne Adufutse

About "You Know Who"

Lights are turning off...muted dogs bark behind doors. A yellow Mustang is blocking the sidewalk. There are no streetlights here and a White guy in a black mini car just offered me a ride home. As I eat the Dunkin glazed doughnut replacement and wish I lived in a more nicely decorated home with you I grow sad.

I feel like I should be living with you. Oh, yes. I have tried to shut you out...your smile and receding short locks. And I had a nice argument with an evil friend who is more jealous than kind. That? Added more to the spice to an otherwise boring beautiful last days of summertime.

Is there a replacement for you? How fast can he get here? They should have hotlines for things such as these—new love replacements. Now that would be more popular than any chat-line or late night television show.

Call me a cornball but driving the latest car and rocking the latest designer jeans just don't do it for me anymore. I'd rather be lying next to you feeling your breath against the heat of my neck—the spot that amusingly torments and makes my thighs laugh.

Are you some kind of cruel disaster bearer? You've swung me to such high and lows. You've disappointed and disappeared like the zit on my forehead. Just like the black spot once red spot above my eyebrow, your trace is still imprinted upon.

Kamikaze of Songs

Am I stupid for loving you so? You are so stuck on things more saccharinely futile than strong and lasting.

But that too, I understand. We each must find our way…some later, others earlier or never. I still feel you are some grand and glorious Malibu sunlight; I would like to keep you that way forever within my imagination. It may be better to let you go once again now. Better to keep the memories less bitter. More of this madness may make me more sour. And life is never lovable when everything is only bitter.

Mianne Adufutse

Rejection

What do you have to do to get love—to be in love, I mean?

Like what?

Love said become thicker, and that I did. But I see love with skinny all day.

Love I hear, likes mean… But I already did that and I'm still all by myself here.

Love is gentle and kind and sweet, right?
So I dolled up 3 love letters in ink that was quite pretty and did everything short of wrapping those letters up in lace.

Love?
Do you like food? Because I can cook. Ask me for almost anything other than minestrone or lentil soup made from scratch and I will do that for you.

Love!
What is it that you want from me?
What must I do to get a hold of you?
I talk a lot on the phone… Is that the hold up? Do you like more introverted ones?

Will candles and cake suit you much better?
I haven't set a table with either of the like in years…

Where Art Thou?

Love?
Am I just that bad? Do you truly hate me so?
Will I be too weathered when you finally stop by to give you my all? Is it that I am bad for real and just don't know it? Is it that I am too good at nothing at all?

Love? What is it with you and me? Why can't we ever seem to get along? Then again, we've never run into each other—not the romantic you!

Love,
I keep on trying to love you even though I don't know who you are, Eros...

Why do I even love you at all?

Mianne Adufutse

Good Careers That Sometime Get Overlooked

Being:
- a race car driver
- an ice skater
- a bellydancer
- a modern dancer--f all this stripper stuff. There are other forms of dance that are beautiful
- a hip-hop dancer--but not ballet. They already get extra hype in the art world
- a writer—a real one, not that 'I wanna write a book to make some quick cash' stuff. I'm talking about a real writer who reads more than they watch television; they type of person who will sit for hours writing and rewriting stuff and still not think it is good enough before they finally complete the 30th manuscript and realize it is good work
- a good singer
- an actor (they get away with everything)
- a voice over specialist
- a talker or a commentator
- a good wife
- a gourmet chef
- a swimmer
- an abstract artist
- an astronaut
- a good listener

Kamikaze of Songs

Getting Rid Of A Bad Thing

Thoughts of you keep molesting my breasts,
it's time to scrub my chest of you;
it's time to rinse the triangle hairs of you.

Fake as good as a candy apple,
deceitfully bad little fortune cookie,
it's time to brush my teeth of you;
it's time to wash my lips of you.

Mud man you still stain like blood
…so vain.

One Person to Avoid

Why is it some people try to pretend you are the one who is crazy when you confront them on some bull they've pulled on you?

They do the most hating-est crap then try to act as though they never did anything to you when you call it to their attention...

Kamikaze of Songs

Haven't Talked to "You Know Who" Since Sunday & Haven't Seen Him in 5+ Weeks

(the text message)

Called you Monday to try to come over but you didn't answer and never called me back. Just words, that I can come over stuff—you didn't mean it really. They say the worst thing a girl can do is tell a guy she really likes him—apparently so. They say initially it is an ego booster for the guy then it turns into a major turn off. Supposedly men love to chase a chick when she is indifferent.

But it doesn't matter now—my feelings for you hang with icicles. Can't keep offering a diamond to someone who doesn't want one. If you have someone close to your heart already or you only like me platonically or you are gay after all, in any event all you had to do was say so instead of being on this regular gaming nigga ish for weeks. I am grown and have no problem moving on. Those are the only reasons I can think of that would cause you to behave like this. I was wrong thinking we had something special. Please do not call me again. I made a big mistake looking you up.

Mianne Adufutse

Wrong One

Even as catastrophic fallen angel boy,
you reign king;
I swim far away from shore
for this thing
--you are lifeguard no more.

Don't know how long I can hang here stranded,
what a quandary
X on my chest,
permanently reprimanded;
I'd advise much better to others

I have clawed out my own heart
…but I used to be smart.
…I used to be smart.

Kamikaze of Songs

8.22.09

1
My lashes keep dropping in my eyes
the tears keep rolling down the sheets

…you won't answer my call that's all
…you won't answer my call…

2
The kids next door play in the backyard happy and singing
and calling for their mom more than their dad

…I wish I could be like that again
…happy
life is no good when happiness is based on someone else
life is no good…

3
Somebody else likes me
but he isn't you
Somebody else likes me
but he doesn't joke around all the time like you do
Somebody else says he loves me all the time
…He loves me all the time, even when I am going on and
on about you and all this stupid bull you constantly pull…

Mianne Adufutse

All The Things I've Missed About You, Mr. Good Man:

- I missed the way you used to make me CD's like Jill Scott and Brian Jackson

- I missed the time you took me to Union Street to eat when you wore your hat cocked to the side

- I missed the way you watched *King of the Hill* that one night when you came back over to sleep next to me

- I missed the way you hooked up my hotmail account back in the day before email was popular

- I missed the way you made me cut hardcore

- I missed the way we danced that one time on the living and dining room floor

- I missed the way you laid on that sweaty leather couch listening to music without trying to score

- I missed the way you spit on it and gave it to me over Twista in your old bedroom

Kamikaze of Songs

- I missed the way you stayed on the phone for 6 hours with me when you were visiting your mom out of town

- I missed the way you always gave me the best, most brand newest looking used books in the bookstore

- I missed your man-hand fingers

- I missed the way you made that one really cute face and pushed up your glasses when you turned serious

- I miss the way you could go from hood to alternative to Mr. Jokeman in nanoseconds

I missed you…
Lost you
then found you…

Now you say you are gay

Now you look like
that pig named Orville off *Garfield* to me
and your nose looks like the crack
of your flat, slouchy ass

- You took me to that skeleton music dungeon where men sandwiched women and nipples were X-ed in masking tape and eyes looked lost in acid vapors

Mianne Adufutse

- You whatever for me, the baby girl

- You say my clit looks like a dick shortly after

- You press ignore when I call you on my birthday

- You take the chicken I stayed in to bake for you and call all mushy thereafter

- You say there aren't too many like me and hide your gay behind the jokes and blunt smokes and welcoming death comments

I do not hate gay men
I do not hate gay women
I only hate you right now --fruity rainbow, skittles boy

You make talk of bitches with a look of the sternness
Simply because you're stuck on some older man with an
old school name--probably something like Ernest

I still love you--just wish you wouldn't
have played me like a presidential puppet;
what I get for being real, I guess
I will go back and steal the old me,
empty canister, inside even less
no longer a kaleidoscope

you are not the same anyway
32 all you do is talk about dope

Kamikaze of Songs

never liked that type—
they are worse than high fructose corn fruit punch
24 you were un-ignorant and teaching
and your thoughts were far reaching
and you bought me lunch and never wanted to let me go
but back to now: sweet on the low; greedy bi hoe,
for this is good gone good-bye!

Mianne Adufutse

Final Adieu

It should be easier
you should have long since left me alone
yet you keep doing this trying to not claim you are a gay
when you know you are a flaming homobisexual fat boy.

I am just as wicked too
like promising never to call again and then I do
I do too much
trying to get back with you
trying to get even with you
trying to hope you will never again say you are gay
then turn around and say it was all in play.

You try to make it so not easy for me
you're trying to give me a hard time on this
come back to your grind
I must not be that easy for you to shake either
I make you remember ladies
I make you remember when…

It should be easier
to stop with all the soggy I love you's
and to shut each other down.
I fear nothing
except that I might get turned to stone for this,
you were not my fate from phase I

a week later you pick up the phone

Kamikaze of Songs

I say I'm so threw but there you go
calling me boo not one time but two

People try to talk me out of my feelings, they say you may not be gay.

In turn I ask,
what straight Black dude
constantly refers to a clit as a dickhead?
A gay. That's all I have to say.

Mianne Adufutse

Done

Over you
glad we're threw
you are something
I'll never again do

Punk fist
show up one more time here,
and you gone be on a funeral list.

Kamikaze of Songs

Be Cool (Lyrics)

Be cool baby
Baby be cool
Be cool baby
Baby be cool
Be cool, be cool, be cool, be cool, be cool, be cool, baby

Naysayers they hate
and they demonstrate when you show them
you don't care what they say, what they think of you
you're gonna be okay

Oh how I know, cause there they go, "She's so stuck up,
she's a hoe, maybe she's mentally slow!"
Trying to add, subtract and multiply
all of the, all of the reasons why
I keep my cool, baby,
I keep it cool, baby

I be cool, I be cool
Oh, oh, how I
I be cool, I be cool
Oh, oh, oh

Mianne Adufutse

Really Love (Lyrics)

I really love you, love you past the physical,
past the physical, past the physical, oh
I really, love you, love you, past the physical

ain't no blackcard got to be involved, no Benz
and you got way less than your mans
but I really love you, love you
past the physical, past the physical

Kamikaze of Songs

Clean Restrooms

Clean restrooms are very important. If you go to a restaurant and the restroom is dirty, you should probably not eat there.

That is why I now will try The Olive Garden off Gratiot in East Pointe. Or is it Roseville?

I had to tinkle so bad. But one cannot go in just any public place. I had held it so long I knew it boiled down to one thing: find a place and go—immediately.

Olive Garden was right there so I went in. And much to my delight, the restrooms were right at the door. And they were clean—like glistening clean!

I will try a dinner at the Olive Garden now. Before that I did not like them. I had only gone there one time when I was a kid and hated it. But now I will have to eat there.

There is a place downtown in Greektown that I used to like to go to. But after one bad memory and seeing how dirty it was there, no amount of good lamb chops and tomato sauce will woo me into eating there again—their ladies restroom was filthy. And so was that one restroom in Mexican village. But Xochimilco's ladies restroom was fairly clean. So that's another good restaurant to dine at if you like Mexican.

Absurd

Kamikaze of Songs

A sign at the driveway entrance of a heath clinic on Detroit's eastside.
Trust

People walk around with their guards up. They let you know up front that they don't trust anybody. "I don't really trust people," they say.

I hear it so much. But guess what?

You have to trust the people that put the bridges together each time you ride on the tollway/freeway. And there are a lot of mini bridges and passages along those roads.

You have to trust whoever paved the streets when you are driving in your car down the road or walking or rolling your wheelchair down the street. The only people who don't have to trust the street pavers are the recluses who choose to stay shut in their homes. Even then, the recluse has to trust whoever built their home. They have to trust that it won't just cave in for no apparent reason on them one day. They have to trust that the foundation of their home was strongly built and that the inspectors were not drunk or high when they checked it and the recluse has to trust that the inspectors were not paid off to certify that their house was well built if in fact it was not well built.

We have to trust other people to some degree on the road when we are driving. Pedestrians have to trust that the drivers will not hit them.

Mianne Adufutse

We have to trust the builders of grocery stores and shopping plazas also. We eat what we bring home from the grocery store trusting that it is not toxic or that the ingredients are exactly what the labels say they are.

We trust that no one will bring a gun into the movie theater and randomly shoot it up.

We trust that the pilot knows how to fly the aircraft when we get on a plane and fly off to some beautiful vacation spot.

Trust.
We do it 24 hours a day.
But then people want to go around saying they don't trust anybody.

Kamikaze of Songs

Good At Things

I cannot keep phone chargers, I am too rough. I break them when I am in the tub and on the phone while it is charging. And I am also good at getting water into phones for this very same reason.

Mianne Adufutse

Personal Bugs

Why do people like to get right up in someone else's face when talking to them?

I don't know, I think everyone has their very own personal bugs and personally I feel like, a person should stand a healthy distance and keep their bugs to themselves. And I will stand at a healthy distance away from you and keep mine to myself. I do not like people getting too close within my personal space unless they are close friends or my man or my dog, Mr. Tag Along or nice looking men.

Kamikaze of Songs

No Regular, Common Chick

To look at her you'd never know she makes returns to the dollar store or that she colors her own hair—she's more expensive looking and intimidating to the guys that still live at home with their mamas. She is also the type that still sits on the swings at the parks; she lies in her backyard and watches the clouds go by on her days off work. She is the one who chased the leprechaun with the rest of the indigo children only to find the pot of gold.

Mianne Adufutse

Sub Regular Chick

She is the type no one misses when she is not around. Her mother, her brother, her best so-called friends, her multiple one-night stands—nobody misses her when she is not around. So she does things to try to make herself useful. Like throwing baby showers for girls she barely knows. Meanwhile, at the baby shower, she flirts with their boyfriends and husbands and will sleep with them at later dates if given the chance. Also, on her days off work, she watches Jerry Springer and reality television shows and goes to get her nails done and hangs out with a dude she has been sleeping with for 14 years. He refuses to marry her. She continues paying when they go out to eat and she continues to pick him up from his girlfriend's house.

The Thing of Life

You have arrived when you can be yourself 24/7.

Now that doesn't mean be intentionally antagonistic or that one must behave the exact same in all situations. A normal person is not going to behave in the same manner at a corporate event as they would a family reunion. We all have more than one personality; humans are multifaceted. There is a side we show to the world, a side we only disclose to close friends and family and then there is a side we keep to ourselves.

Mianne Adufutse

Hair Issue

I wore weave for years—like 15 years or more. And individual lashes way before any non-Hollywood-er was wearing them on a regular basis. Last year I cut and relaxed my hair. It was cute some said, but they liked the weave better.

Now I wear a blonde fro. I get so many compliments from White girls and men of all races. But Black women? OMG! They dog the mess out of the do! All it is is a blonde Afrohawk. If it was relaxed the Black girls wouldn't be hating on it. The Black girls working at Charlotte Russe were saying my hair was a hot mess. Well, I think their boring relaxed wraps are dripping in boredom. Conformists. Can anyone around here think for themselves?

Even in Hollywood, it's amazing how everyone follows suit. As I type this, anybody who is anybody of A-list sistas are wearing black hair coloring. And it's either long and layered or short like a Halle or Rihanna do. Cassie and Amber Rose are the only ones I see doing something original with their hair.

So I am recording this now so that in 5-10 years, when all these other Black girls start rocking Afrohawks and other Afroflavored hairdo's there will be no doubt I was doing it already way back when—while they were trying to dog me out for it.

Really, when the Black girls hate on my hair, all they are saying is, "Gee, I don't have the guts to wear my hair like that!"

I already conformed back in 2007 when one of my then best friend/homegirls hated on my sistalocks. And more than a few relatives did not like the locks either. But this time I shall stand strong. I like my hair and I like being able to wake up and go.

But anyway, why do Black people claim to be so Pro-Black then turn around and say naps are horrible. On the Black gossip websites they have a picture of Beyonce with a healthy inch of new growth around the edges. They said, "This is unacceptable!"

Why are we still visiting the hair issue in 2009?

Black folks, I love you but the road is a long one ahead—especially for Negroes like yung berg talking about he doesn't like dark skinned women or "dark butts" as he calls them.

Mianne Adufutse

The Ones

When the eyes shine, so do The Great Ones.

You will know them when you see them. They are the ones hard at work on their earthly assignments. They smile and are happy no matter what people say about them. They take care of their business, are on top of their game and try to help others as much as they can.

But they do not deal with everyone closely. Dealing closely with everyone means giving everyone a chance to get over on them—they are very giving, The Great Ones.

Most of the times people do not even know just how Great they are. And they take The Great Ones for granted.

The next time you see someone with shining eyes—not from liquor or anything like that but with a genuine love for life, watch how you treat them—for they are one of our Greats.

Kamikaze of Songs

Him

Soulmate Central, the Star Dip, for he is mine and I am his.

Leap Frog told me the other day that he did not look deeply into the soul of that one girl who hurt him. With him, it was other issues. He thought he could manipulate that young girl and ended up finding himself caught in the mouth of a Nahusha. But both of them could very well be well-meaning snakes in that situation.

With me, I was stuck on "Sorry I didn't call" and "Sorry I don't like you at all." And also stuck on "Love is on her deathbed." When, in all actuality, you are the one for me. I think.

If you are not the one for me then, "Love is stuck between quick poisonous thrills and worries of late payment of bills." And in that case then my buddy is right, "Cupid did die and leave us."

Mianne Adufutse

Meditate & Procreate

The garbage disposal has not been working for a while and I had the darnedest time finding my heart pendant necklace.

So I meditated and visualized the sink working just fine and the necklace in my hand.

Three days later and I can honesty say my sink works and my necklace is in my jewelry box now. I lifted the mail off the kitchen counter and found my necklace. Today I flipped on the garbage disposal button and, to my delight, it worked.

Mr. Awesome!!!

You are awesome—everything I put on my list as far as what kind of personality I desired in a man. I can actually have real conversations with you--you know something about everything—from the name of the fish that walk on land to what state laws have been amended. And you're still hood! It's crazy! I just can't believe it. And you spoil the mess out of me…

You are awesome--the perfect blend for my personality. And your laugh makes me laugh.

Much love dude. Just don't start acting crazy on me down the road or you will have to go!

Mianne Adufutse

Nerve Racking

- Black people need to start leaving reasonable tips when they dine out. Almost all cell phones these days have a tip calculator somewhere within their menu. Use it. Tip. Or don't go out to eat. They wear expensive hair, nails and clothes making True Religion and Enyce rich but don't wanna tip the very person serving them their food.

- People need to stop wasting food. I see a lot of people go out to eat and barely eat their food. And they don't try to take the leftovers in a doggie bag. It's not like the people I'm talking about are rich, either. Then they don't want to tip. If you can afford to waste food, you can afford to tip, goddammit!

- People need to stop driving for a whole mile with their turn signal blinker on.

Kamikaze of Songs

How They Do

Since February they have lynched Chris Brown. I am not for the domestic violence scene AT ALL. But how on earth, how on earth do actors have the nerve to sign a petition to forgive Roman Polanski for *raping* a 13 year old girl in 1977? He moved to Switzerland to escape that situation and has since committed a similar crime. But! They want to pardon *him*!

Then, a guy murdered a man and guess what? He only went to jail for 24 days! 24 days! Chris Brown loses contracts, he gets publicly tarred and feathered and lynched and Roman, what? The man who killed somebody, what? NOTHING BUT 24 DAYS!!!

Then you have correction officers in jails and prisons raping the female inmates but nobody talks about that…

Mianne Adufutse

Wing Heaven

So there's this place on Gratiot and 7 mile—a chicken place and they sell kool aid, ribs, fish and shrimp dinners. It's Black owned and their slogan is:
> *Only the good chickens go in*!

The girl working in there just said, "9 minutes and we out dis bitch, what!"

Kamikaze of Songs

Hate It

I have been bumping into brick walls all summer. Now, I don't see people anymore, just the white broken dashes painted down the roads.

Somewhere there is a place for me. A place I can really live. And listen to Portishead and Bjork and not have to deal with people who really know nothing other than the wrong things they have been taught. Here, around these parts, it is hard to find another who listens Sam Sparro's "Black and Gold" and Imani Coopla's "Key's to Your Ass" and symphony orchestras or national public radio.

They think they know so much but many places are country and stuck in backward thinking. Some are so stuck on being common conformists. Some Black folks really are intolerant of others.

If being well rounded, if being non conforming to wrong theories or teaching that do not fit my mental make-up makes me strange to the common populace, so be it because there are way more places to live than here.

That is why I have a love-hate relationship with simpletons. Many are afraid to think for themselves. The old are afraid of the young and the young don't respect the old.

In the inner cities across America everyone is on the same hustle: either bootlegging real artists' music and movies or real estate hustles wherein they get a raggedy house and try to fix it up to put someone in it on section 8 or else they are petty low budget drug dealers or they become self-made preachers.

Well meaning people invite me to their church to talk about my book but I don't out of respect. Jesus turned the tables of the Pharisees over for vending in the temple. For me personally I don't feel comfortable selling things at church. The crosses around the necks is a bit touchy to me as well. If I had a child that got killed on a cross or by a gun or any other weapon, I would not wear it around my neck. That would be an added offense. But that is a personal decision.

The average Black Detroiter needs to pay attention to what is going on in Africa at the hands of China right now. I hardly know any young Black Detroit men who read the newspaper. Even though the news is sometimes filled with propaganda, some of the brothas in the hood need to check it out.

Everyday I hear of someone getting killed in Detroit or going to jail. And at the clubs there is almost at least one So & So Just Got Out of Jail party. It's sad. All across America the hood is still the hood.

Kamikaze of Songs

Detroit in particular has the nations top crime rate yet it has the most churches empirically out of the whole nation. I just don't say anything now when Black folks tell me they don't read anything other than the bible. They actually think that sounds good to say. There is nothing wrong with reading the bible and it is very important to be spiritually sound but one has to keep abreast of the things going on in the world around them. There is nothing wrong with reading the bible and other things as well.

Mianne Adufutse

Why?

Why do some Black folks say they are proud to be Black yet they will still dog a person for being really dark?

Why do the same Black folks who say they hate White folks *prefer* light skin and light-eyes?

Why do some Black folks I know who have college degrees still think Africa is a country?

Reconnecting With An Old *Supposed To Be* Friend

I am not trying to right my wrongs anymore. That happens when one tries to change fate. Changing the fated way things are destined to happen only slams your face into the ice-cold sidewalk and sets you back.

Mianne Adufutse

The Begging Woman At The Strip Mall Who Curses People Out

Some say she is crazy, some tell her to seek The Lawd. She is on something and maybe just playing crazy for the heck of it.

She holds the credit union doors open and harasses patrons into giving her money. I had decided to feel sorry for her until the time the police came and she yelled at them for not making me leave along with her.

How does a woman get to that point?

One time she had on a twisted, matted wig and some women walked by and complimented her on it. Usually she just wears a short, matted, linty natural.

This is why I don't see why there are so many urban books and raps about the drug game. Its causes and effects can be seen 24/7. There are other things to write about or rap about other than drug addicts and drug dealers all the time.

I wonder how drug dealers can sell stuff that lets people get themselves to the point this woman has reached. But then again, to ban drug dealers would be to ban all U.S. pharmacies and pharmacists.

Kamikaze of Songs

And to ban all local, urban drug dealers and to un-glorify and un-glamorize being a drug dealer would mean there would be more Black men available for more Black women and the rise of functioning Black families.

Mianne Adufutse

Lower Mental Socio Economic Status

I make it a point to tell little Black kids that they are handsome or pretty and that they can become anything positive they want to be. Many times their parents look at me extra strange and say things like, "No, she ain't! She bad!" Or, "He ain't gone do nothing. Not wit dem grades! He don't like school!"

Being Too Nice…

His mother came to where I lived at the time and called me evil and a fake writer. She had her teeth in this time. Then she said she was his wife—his mother said she was his wife.

He and I got into it because of that episode. All he had to do was tell her not to come over with that mess. But he wouldn't. So she kicked up a tornado in my house with her tongue. Surprised it didn't get violent. Some mamas are so in love with their sons…

Then, I took him back. And he ogles other women around me like I am one of the boys. But he has no car, a shaky job and awkward breath.

Why am I so nice?

Why am I too nice?

So this, too, is over.

Celibacy is underrated.

Mianne Adufutse

East Side Strip

Where I first started selling books…

Sea Creature

Why is it that lately the guys that like me look like land and sea creatures? Then I was out selling my books and this guy had on a shirt that said **Land & Sea Creatures** in the upper left-hand corner of his chest. Weird.

Mianne Adufutse

Facebook, Myspace & Twitter

Okay, so I admit it, I used to be on Myspace blogging and all the rest of it. But then I stopped. Think about it. All it is is a bunch of people and celebrities telling all their business.

When I tell people this fact, they say, "Who cares?"

So I hope the day never comes when they try to put chips in our arms. Or when their job mandates that they get Swine Flu vaccinations like they are currently doing in some New York hospitals. And I hope the day never comes when personal checking accounts are frozen and the New World Order is complete.

Kamikaze of Songs

In Style

Everyone is wearing skulls on their tee shirts somewhere. I even see infants with outfits covered in skeleton heads.

And with good timing. Currently the masses have taken their own brains out of their skulls and thrown them in the nearby trashcan. Clothing exemplified.

Mianne Adufutse

On the G20

There was the G7 back in the day. They are the ones responsible for the Great Scramble For Africa. European countries knew the land was rich in resources and decided to take it from its inhabitants.

Right now the G7 still exists. They call the leaders of its pack "ministers."

And the G20 is the financial central banking system. Or, "finance ministers."

The average adult I meet on the street knows nothing about this. But they can tell you the color of Mary J. Bliges new 'do (nothing wrong with Mary—I'm just saying); what store has Ed Hardy pants on sale; all the names of the *Desperate Housewives*; and where to get the best deal on fruit. Genetically modified fruit. Only a lot of people don't even know it's genetically engineered. And if you told them, they'd be indifferent anyway.

It's exactly how elitists planned it.

Kamikaze of Songs

The Original Greatest High School of 1995

In 2009

Mianne Adufutse

As The Slaves Turn In Their Graves

Today, for the first time in 4 months I watched television. On Bet 106 and Park they have this thing where they show viewer's texts in the lower left corner as a video plays.

Now, I am all for text abbreviations just like the next person. But the texts the Black kids were sending were all misspelled and loaded with bad grammar. Why did BET put that on there like that? People already think Black folks are stupid. And that is not helping the problem. You want to raise the matriculation rate in urban educational systems? Stop putting that bad grammar crap on television like it's acceptable on Black networks! Stuff like that is only encouraging stupidity.

The slaves were not even allowed to read. Now we have the opportunity to become anything we want but too many of us want to revel in being dumb and don't want to learn anything.

The Great Move to California

Day three: On the bus there was a redneck who kept saying the N word and then apologizing. He stood right next to the African American bus driver and would repeatedly ask to be dried out as he writhed violently back and forth.

Day four: On the bus coming from Van Nuys, the White boy kept saying the N word loudly and talking to his friends about how his mother was scared of Black folks. None of the Black folks on the bus uttered a word. I turned around and looked at him wishing to knock his head off with my oversized blue bag. He looked mixed.

Day six: The Mexican man said the N word when I walked pass.

Mianne Adufutse

19

Photo taken by Adrianne Adufutse

Kamikaze of Songs

Grandma Afua

Mianne Adufutse

I used to stare at her picture when I was a kid a lot. Still to this day I find her face pleasantly interesting. My other grandmother looks like she is silly like me but chooses to hide it in elegant photo poses. I wonder if her voice was deep. I wonder if I have more in common with her other than her chin and the way she holds her hand on this picture and our Afua Adufutse names. I think she was very pretty and that we'd have gotten along and that I could have learned a lot from her. Some people, though they are old, have nothing to teach anyone other than how not to be. With her, I know she'd have something to tell me. Things I never would have forgotten. Things that would have made life easier in the past.

Other books by Mianne Adufutse

Even If You Don't...
A contemporary urban, neoclassic suspenseful romance compiled of erotica, paranormal happenings, social commentary & humor
Mi Books

Everything In Style Should Not Be Worn
A collection of poetry, plays, social/magical and surreal realism pieces
Flippynerds Imprint

Just Talking To You Because There Is No One Else To Talk To: My Journal & Other Outrageous Things
~collection 2
Flippynerds Imprint

Vert Means More Than Green
Very Explicit Real Talk
From astrology to relationship advice with a straight up freak nasty bent and a dash of light humour, Vert is a quirky stop-n-start, nouvelle kind of read.
Flippynerds Imprint

Mianne Adufutse

Upcoming works:

Children's books—Lights On Art

A short story collection

Please check our site for upcoming releases & readings www.flippynerds.com

email questions or comments regarding this publication to flipnerd@flippynerds.com

Books can also be ordered in stores or on:
Bn.com
Amazon.com

www.ingramcontent.com/pod-product-compliance
Lightning Source LLC
LaVergne TN
LVHW041543060526
838200LV00037B/1117